DIAL M FOR MONKEY

DIAL M FOR MONKEY

ADAM MAXWELL

tonto press

www.tontopress.com

A TONTO PRESS PUBLICATION 2006

First published in 2006 by Tonto Press

ISBN 0-9552183-2-2
978-0-9552183-2-3

Cover design and artwork John Hardy
with thanks to Robin Brown

Tonto Press
Blaydon on Tyne
United Kingdom

www.tontopress.com

10 9 8 7 6 5 4 3 2 1

For Eve

CONTENTS

HAPPINESS IS A WARM GUN

I WASN'T sure if I'd dug the grave deep enough. After all, he was tall as me. But here, under the willow tree he loved so much, seemed a fitting place to bury him. He would have wanted it this way.

There is very little I am sure of in this life, but following the literal advice of a man who had once claimed to be a Walrus was not the beginning of an adventure I might someday tell my grandchildren. Even as I pressed the start button on the microwave I should have known it would end in disaster.

And so here I was, with the weeping willow's sharp branches stinging the top of my head, jabbing into me as I continued digging. It was more tiring than I would have expected but it felt somehow satisfying as the spade sliced clinically into the soft earth of my garden.

I had only set the microwave to cook for four minutes but even that was three minutes and sixteen seconds too long. It felt right, at the time, to test the theory, to see if John Lennon meant it literally or metaphorically. Now the words rang hollow in my ears.

I watched from the other side of the kitchen as the microwave sprung to life, the turntable inside rotating the pistol and the familiar hum of convenience cookery. Perhaps I should have taken out the bullets. With a whirr the machine rotated its deadly dish, animated but unaware of the potential implications of nuking this 9mm entrée.

After fifteen seconds I retreated to the hallway, poking my head around the door just enough to see what would happen. I giggled under my breath as the adrenalin began to trickle into my system.

Thirty seconds, and the sparks were flying inside the glass door.

Forty seconds, and Paul, my Irish Wolfhound, sprinted down the hall, into the kitchen and skidded to a halt on the polished floor looking at me and panting heavily. I leaped forward to grab him but, all of a sudden: *bang, bang, shoot, shoot.*

Paul was indeed dead.

SHOOTING JELLY WITH A SHOTGUN

'OW! Shit! I think a bee stung my ear!'

'Fucking hell, Charlie. Your ear's bleeding!'

'What? Oh my God!'

Charlie passed out before I reached him. As I approached his crumpled body I could see the widening crimson patch seeping through the fibre of his t-shirt. I gagged, I admit it. I doubled over, my hands grabbing my knees and my eyes closed. An icy sweat climbed up my back and, as I opened my eyes, I could see a chunk of Charlie's ear lying a couple of feet away.

Becoming a victim of a stray nail from a careless carpenter's nail gun changed Charlie. The realisation that, if the nail had been two inches to the left, he could have lost an eye, or worse. He had been working as a bricklayer on a couple of contracts with me, and would never wear a hard-hat, instead preferring his own brand of lax sloppiness. Now he slept in the fucking thing. Losing half an ear will do strange things to a man.

A few weeks later we had a job laying foundations. Me and Charlie were on a break and, without any warning, he was catapulted backwards across the site in a puff of masonry dust.

For a moment I stared at the space he had just occupied. There were little specs of dust floating in the air. It was then my mind began processing the accompanying noise.

It had sounded like someone shooting a jelly with a shotgun and then, a split second later, a sledgehammer hitting a porcelain toilet.

Everyone knows that bones break when they're hit too hard, they're weak under extreme pressure and can splinter and break as easily as twigs.

Bones, however, are not dead wood. Every cell in your body is constantly being replaced by new living tissue and your bones are no different. At the hospital later that day I was surprised when the doctor told me that the pelvis is made up of three bones that grow together as people age; the ilium, ischium and pubis. On each side of the pelvis there is a hollow cup, the acetabulum which serves as a socket for the hip joints.

I turned to look behind me. Charlie lay, a concrete block embedded between his splayed legs, separating his ilium from his ischium and his pubis from his acetabulum. The doctors later told me his hips had both been pushed out of socket as his pelvis shattered.

It got worse.

His poor mangled pelvis had absorbed the majority of the blow and had cracked just like the breaking porcelain toilet sound which had echoed around the building site. It troubled me all the way to the hospital when I found out what the other sound was.

It is a fairly well known fact in most circles that if a man is kicked between the legs then the results will be pain, shock, confusion and sometimes even nausea. Kick hard enough and you can tag vomiting and an inability to walk to the list. The blood vessels which supply the testicles through the hole in the middle of the pelvis will burst and begin to bleed internally into the scrotum.

If, for arguments sake, a large concrete block swings loose and strikes you between the legs, doctors will tell you that a testicular rupture may occur. This is when the testicle is compressed against the pubic bone with such force that it is crushed.

The doctors will tell you this. What they won't tell you is that it sounds like shooting jelly with a shotgun.

JIM MORRISON'S LEG

I STOLE Oscar Wilde's cock you know,' said Jamie.

'No you didn't,' I said. 'You just told me you'd never done this before.'

'I haven't. But you know that massive statue of an angel?'

My shoulders ached as the spade pushed into the ground once more. It only took a month of working in the Pere Lachaise to get this far. Paris' most famous cemetery, the resting place of such luminaries as Edith Piaf and Oscar Wilde, had eagerly taken me on. In fact such an impression had been made I felt confident my employers would forgive the minor indiscretion currently being perpetrated. I put down the spade as I reached softer soil, took off my cap, wiped the sweat from my brow, and tossed the useless garment onto the tombstone of the grave I was digging up.

'Please tell me that you didn't reduce one of history's finest literary minds to the level of a knob gag…' I trailed off, knowing only too well where this conversation was going.

'That's right! I got in here, chiselled it off, and sold it on eBay.' Jamie took another swig from the bottle of wine that seemed to permanently reside in his overall pocket.

The Pere Lachaise stretched out around us like an orchestra, the arrondissements cutting through the pit with great sweeps separating the violinist from the cellist and the famous from the infamous.

'Shut up and keep digging,' I launched the shovel into the earth and, with a crack that echoed in the purple night, I struck a rock. The handle sheared, leaving half in my hand and half wedged into the ground.

'Ah shit!'

Jamie started laughing.

'For God's sake shut up. I'll have to go and get another one now.'

'At this time of night?'

'Yes. At this time of night. Listen, I'll go to the gatehouse and grab one from the gardener's supplies. I've got the keys in my bag.'

I hauled myself out of the pit we had created, the loose

soil around the edges crumbling back down and making more work for us. I stared for a moment at Jamie as he continued digging. 'Keep at it, I'll be back as soon as I can.'

Walking away, the sound of Jamie whistling some tuneless dirge he had picked up in the café down the street grated. The notes hung in the air like my breath. Staring too long at middle C, I stumbled forward, tripping on something hard underfoot. The world rushed towards me but I reached out and stopped myself at the last moment. With a clatter, the contents of my top pocket spilled onto the ground.

I got up, reached forward, and scooped the decrepit old harmonica into my cold hands. It had been silver once but the corroded turd that squatted in my palm was nothing more than a tarnished reminder of my father's wasted life. My father: the dreamer, the failed musician, the man who had tried out for The Doors but was told in no uncertain terms by Jim Morrison himself that he was next to useless. I had taken it from my father's house on the day of his funeral.

The door to the gatehouse was typical of everything about the Pere Lachaise: grandiose while managing somehow to look ramshackle. I turned the key and the familiar grinding of the gears I had heard every morning since starting work here rang out. I tried to slip inside quietly, hiding behind my shadow, but the door had other ideas, crying out into the night, its ancient wood creaking with resentment.

It was surprisingly cold inside. My feet crunched across the flagstones as I moved swiftly through the building and up the stairs. It didn't take me long to locate a new spade but as I was about to make my way back downstairs a noise stopped me in my tracks.

The door downstairs, the one I had carefully locked behind me, was creaking again, the rusted hinges echoing throughout the gatehouse. It couldn't be Jamie, he didn't have a key.

My ears burned hot as the blood rushed to them and turned the footsteps that echoed from downstairs into a pounding drum in my head. I had to hide. They couldn't find me. Not now. It wasn't supposed to happen this way.

I moved quickly and silently. The footsteps were definitely getting louder, moving upstairs towards me. A second later I was in the tool cupboard, hastily pulling the door closed behind me and trying not to knock over the spades and hoes inside.

My breath had quickened its tempo, moving to staccato, the vapour more obvious in the moonlit room. I pushed myself further back into the cupboard, clutching the harmonica hard in my hand. The door to the room swung open and the light flicked on as the walls of my hiding place began to close in.

'Of course I'll help you,' Jamie had said at the top of his voice.

'Please shhhhh,' I gestured to all the other people in the café.

'They're all fucking French – no-one understands a word we're saying. Do you?' he stood up and addressed the café as a whole, squinting at the sun dancing in through the bay windows. 'Does anyone here speak English?'

One or two hands went up, some words were muttered and then more were tentatively pushed into the air. After a few seconds the café was full of raised hands.

'Ah. Okay then, let's go. So what was it that you wanted to tell me that was so secret anyway?'

Jamie may have been lacking a lot of traits, but dependability certainly wasn't one of them, and it was this I was relying on for the task ahead.

'You see, Jamie,' I said as the door of the café shut behind us.

'They've always been the same if you ask me,' he interrupted.

'There's this thing I've been thinking about doing.'

'All eating their fucking croissants and being so bloody aloof.'

'I think it's the only way I can start to move forward as

a musician.'

'Music? Don't talk to me about music – all they bloody listen to is that sodding Edith Piaf…'

'Well not just as a musician. As a person as well.'

'I tell you what, Dan, if I ever get the chance I'm gonna take a piss on that woman's grave.'

'I'm sure that will help,' I snapped. 'Now listen I need your help.'

And so I told him. I glossed over some of it. Made it sound like the sort of student prank we used to play, but for the most part I told him the truth. How I wanted to go to the Pere Lachaise and pay the late Jim Morrison a visit. How I wanted to take his femur and have it made into a trumpet.

'You are a good trumpet player,' Jamie nodded in agreement.

'It's a Tibetan thing. Apparently the bone's sound is so deep it has a resonance you just can't imagine.'

'I can imagine.'

'No, it's not just that.'

There was a pause and we looked at each other for a moment.

'It's your Dad isn't it?'

I nodded.

'Anything to get one over on these Frenchies mate,' he said.

'Jamie, you've lived here for eight years and your fian-cée is French. Please shut up.'

Back in the incendiary void of the cupboard, things weren't going quite so well. We didn't have a contingency plan for getting caught.

'Yeah, I told you,' said Gerry, one of my co-workers. 'I've just got to find my house keys and then I'll pick you up.'

Footsteps clattered by, circling the room, with Gerry occasionally pausing to rummage in a bag or box. I tried to crane my neck, to see if the light that was breaking in illuminated any keys around me.

'No sweetie, I really mean it. Of course I'm not with another woman, that's ridiculous.'

It was only a matter of seconds before I would be dis-covered. If only I hadn't hidden in the cupboard. At least then I could have got away with pretending I had fallen asleep.

'I'll be right over as soon as I – aha!'

I waited, not daring to breathe, to move, or even blink. I stared at the crack in the door.

'Yes. Oui. Oui. C'est ça ma petite lapin.'

The light went out, the door shut and I exhaled.

'Where the hell have you been?'

I waved the new spade at him and he waved his wine at me in return.

'I decided to stop.'

'What?' I shouted. 'We haven't got time for you to stop!'

'Calm down. I had to stop for two reasons. Firstly because I needed a piss.'

'Oh you didn't,' I asked, scared of the response but knowing it all the same. 'Please tell me you didn't…'

'I did,' he grinned. 'I pissed on Edith Piaf's grave!'

'Jamie!'

'And secondly, cos I think we're nearly there.'

'Shit! Are you serious?'

I scrambled into the grave, shovel in hand, and started digging. Within a matter of minutes my spade met with wooden resistance.

'This is it,' I whispered to Jamie who was hovering over the grave mouth.

Soon we had cleared the top of the casket, and the plaque, although tarnished, bore the Lizard King's name.

The crowbar slid easily into my hands as I braced myself against the grave's sides and began levering at the head of the coffin. My hands felt clammy as the wood cracked and splintered, giving way easily to the pressure.

'This is it! This really is it!'

'Open the bloody coffin already and let's get out of

here,' said Jamie. 'Someone's bound to come along eventually you know.'

The lid crackled open, gasses hissing out as the seal that had been made decades earlier was broken.

'Well? Have you got it?'

I hoisted the lid to one side.

'Jamie,' I said. 'I think we have a problem.'

'What do you mean?'

'Well, it seems he's escaped.'

'Shit, you mean someone has beaten us to it?' Jamie passed me a torch and I shone it into the vacant coffin.

'No, I mean that I don't think he was ever...'

I trailed off as the torch glanced upon a small white piece of paper lying halfway down the length of the coffin. Reaching out, I picked it up. It was a business card. On it was printed an address in Paris and three words.

James Douglas Morrison.

It was over and I knew it. I put the business card in my pocket and as the pair of us walked away I took out the harmonica, staring at its rust-encrusted reeds in the pre-dawn light.

I wiped it on my sleeve and then, after a moment put it to my lips and exhaled, inhaled, exhaled. It sounded awful but it reminded me of a Bob Dylan song I couldn't remember the name of.

'Sounds like Chas and Dave that,' said Jamie. 'I miss

Chas and Dave.'

I ALMOST SPANKED A MONKEY

THE Metro train ground to a halt, brakes screaming at a station so far underground it could be the dead-centre of the earth. The doors sighed open and in stepped a man. I thought I had seen him before.

He billowed through the doors, his long black coat a full two seconds behind him, then stepped into the carriage and stopped, giving his coat an opportunity to catch up. His red waistcoat, his yellow and red striped trousers, his moustachioed face, the teeth like a burnt fence... It was only when two small monkeys darted out of the folds of his coat that I realised I *had* seen him before.

A buzzer sounded and the doors slid shut.

'Ladies and gentlemen,' he said with a booming voice.

'I have a rare treat for you today – without a net my monkey here will perform something never before seen on any underground transport system in the world.'

Passengers were staring. *I* was staring. The monkey stood upright, staring back, with only a tiny red waistcoat to cover his modesty.

'Not even the subway in New York has seen such a performance,' he said. 'My little friend here will sing *Superstition* by the genius that is Stevie Wonder. In G sharp.'

Passengers craned their necks, eager to see what the lunatic in fancy dress was shouting about. I was no different and I stumbled forward as the train pulled away.

'Take it away, Terry.'

We all stared at the monkey. He drew himself up onto his back legs, and opened his mouth. The train jolted forward, but he remained upright, baring his fangs and emitting a howl.

Then Terry burst into *Superstition*. Apparently in G sharp.

The other monkey was making his way along the carriage. I watched as he reached a furry fist into a passenger's handbag. He pulled out a purse, then scampered back, stealth-style, to his master. A quick pit-stop in his master's coat and he was off, back down the carriage. The paw flashed out again, this time into the pocket of a skater's low riders. The monkey tugged at the contents, and the jeans slid down slightly.

I could see he had a problem and as I leaned forward, I saw the skater's wallet attached to the jeans by a chain. The monkey was wily, and released the catch before taking the booty, and bolting. While all this was happening, Terry hadn't missed a beat and was keeping a good tune in spite of the fact that it was in G sharp.

His friend, meanwhile, changed direction. Our eyes met and I could feel his panic. I wasn't supposed to be watching him. I was supposed to be marvelling at his mate Terry singing. Everyone else was. He eyed me suspiciously for a moment and then charged across the carriage towards his next target: me.

I wasn't sure how to react to a monkey ambush. My breathing was heavy. I was squinting, focussing, trying to keep that thieving little shit in my sights. I knew then I had to kick that monkey's arse.

Slowly, he stood upright, his miniscule monkey mind processing some long-held instinct. He lifted his right arm, clenching his paw. He froze, fist aloft, and stared deep into my eyes as I waited for his move.

The doors sighed open.

He stared. I stared.

A buzzer sounded. The doors slid shut.

We moved forward, and so did his hand, shooting

down and cupping his fucking monkey nuts. He yanked at them with one paw whilst frantically beating his chest with the other. And then, *whoosh*, he vanished.

And I checked my pockets, on my hands and knees, emptying them onto the floor. I hadn't taken the opportunity to kick his skinny arse when I'd had the chance. And I had paid the price: the man in the black coat, Terry, the light-fingered marmoset, and my wallet. All gone.

A buzzer sounded and the doors slid shut.

THE HOLY FACE OF GARY BARLOW

HE was working a normal job, in his late twenties, name of Thomas. It was delivery day and he was going through the motions of unloading the hardware supplies from the truck. Mundane is a word you could have used to describe the job but that probably wouldn't have done it justice. Mindless would definitely have been a better one, so we'll use that.

It was a mindless job and as a result Thomas' imagination was prone to wander. Not in a 'boy who cried wolf' way. This is not that kind of story. Thomas' imaginings were things he kept to ward off the lure of insanity. Sex with the receptionist. Training an orang-utan to slap every third person who walked through the door. Wondering if cushions were stuffed with foam or whether it was actually specially dried jellyfish. That sort of thing.

So, when he was unloading slices of sheet metal and he saw a face that wasn't a distorted version of his own staring back at him, he was fairly taken aback. Thomas, however, was not the sort of person to let this go easily, and so he parted with ten pounds and took the sheet of metal home, citing a leaky roof in his toilet as the reason.

Over beers and cigarettes with his flatmate Simon, it was decided that unfortunately they had not found a likeness of the Christ. Neither had they found a likeness of the dark one Beelzebub. This piece of sacred sheet metal had been adorned with a likeness of his Holiness Gary Barlow from nineties pop-combo Take That.

At first it seemed highly unlikely, but upon serious Googling they even managed to track down a photograph of Gary in a very similar pose. Six cans of Stella and twice as many phone calls later, the pair were convinced that this could be their meal ticket for the foreseeable future.

And then the pilgrimages started. First female friends, then friends' girlfriends, fiancées, wives. Three days on and the doorbell was ringing every twenty minutes. It was, as Thomas soon commented to Simon, unprecedented.

Thomas had never been a fan of Take That and had actively ridiculed them to both of the girlfriends he had been with during the group's birth right through to their ascension into pop heaven. Indeed, the latter relationship had ended as much for his unwillingness to accept *Could It Be Magic* as 'their song' as for anything else.

Charging visitors to see the Holy face of Gary Barlow seemed to be the next logical step, and so that was exactly what they did. Local press picked it up, then national, then it was all over the internet. Gary Barlow had appeared in sheet metal, and where there was a Holy image there was money to be made.

And then the phone calls started.

Warnings, followed by hang-ups. A man who was softly spoken giving Thomas instructions to close down his little money maker. The two friends stiffened their resolve. They discussed it at length in the pub and came to the conclusion that if either of them discovered their girlfriends were paying money to catch a glimpse of a pop effigy, then they would probably be pissed off enough to make the same sort of phone calls. Assuming they had girlfriends, which, at the present time, they did not.

They were happy with their decision and on the way home bought a kebab each in celebration. As they left the kebab shop, however, they became aware of a figure following them. At first they couldn't be sure. The figure followed the shadows, didn't reveal itself, and they were pretty pissed-up. But within a few hundred yards they knew the figure was in steady pursuit of them. Foolishly they split up, safe in the knowledge that they knew the streets better than their stalker and that he could not follow them both.

He was standing in the doorway when they arrived home. Spoke to them in no uncertain terms. Gave them an ultimatum: hand over the likeness, or face the consequences. What were the consequences?

'You give me the metal or I'll slice off *your* face and smear it on the window. We'll see how many people pay to come and see that.'

The words dripped out carefully, methodically, and were accompanied by the removal of a hunting knife from the depths of the figure's coat. The blade, some seven inches long, reflected the orange street light towards Thomas and Simon.

They nodded in agreement, and the figure stepped aside, allowing them access to their flat, hiding the knife in the folds of his coat and replacing it with a mobile phone into which he uttered just one word. By the time Thomas and Simon arrived with the sheet of metal, a Transit van stood in the road.

The figure stared momentarily at the image in the metal, and his eyebrow flickered in recognition.

'You boys be good now,' he said as he slipped into the passenger door of the Transit.

And like that – the Barlow was gone.

'It looked nothing like him in reality did it?' asked Thomas.

'Nah, not really,' replied Simon. 'But I never realised what a vicious fucker he was.'

ADAM MAXWELL

THE BEGINNING

THE date was going very well as far as Rich was concerned. He had made jokes and Madeline had genuinely laughed. The waiter had a thick Italian accent that matched the thick Italian soup they had for starters and was just this side of patronising. Rich was happy with the progress and, in spite of the fact that he hadn't had a successful date for over six months, had decided to order something without garlic. Rich had never considered himself someone who expected anything on a first date but he had a gut feeling that a snog wasn't out of the question.

This hadn't gone unnoticed by Madeline. As they ordered she had made a mental note that Rich was avoiding her garlic-laden suggestions. Once they had finished the soup she knew she couldn't bear it any longer. The calculated hope or unknown desperation hung in the air in a way that she couldn't ignore. She made a minor excuse and went to the toilet, grabbing her coat on the way.

Madeline had refused to acknowledge this in Rich, despite the fact that she had also completely failed to have a successful date in even longer. She reflected upon this in some detail as she waited for rescue, trapped as she was half-in and half-out of the toilet window. She knew that Rich would probably see her pulling-pants when he eventually came looking for her as they hung in the air in a much more tangible way than his desperation.

SHERRY FOR BREAKFAST

TRAMPS make great friends.

They do not, however, make great pets. Sometimes, if they are raised from puppies, they can be house-trained, but unfortunately this is seldom the case.

Because if they were house-trained they just wouldn't be tramps. A house-trained tramp is no more than an ill-smelling roommate.

But they do make great friends.

They are the philosophers of the street. Have you ever tried, for example, having a conversation with a tramp? I'm not talking about the usual:

'Big Issue?'

'I've already got it this week.'

No, I mean have you ever really taken the time out of your hectic life (and believe me I've seen your schedule – it is *busy*) to get in there – in depth and ask the questions that matter?

'How is it possible,' you may use as your starter for ten, 'to surpass boredom?'

'Whasa maayt?' he may well respond.

'For I, as a member of the television classes, can no longer spend time alone. I sit night after night in front of my high definition entertainment prison, and if more than twelve consecutive moments pass without adequate stimulation, I am bored. Whilst you, my inebriated friend, are able to sit in the park and piss in your second-hand pants without the merest wisp of ennui dancing through your murky mind. Why not come for a drink with me so we may lighten the evening with some talk of Descartes, the singing of a folk song and the imbibing of intoxicating liquor?'

'Nowthasundmerlakit.'

An accord of sorts may be reached whereby you can regale one another with the aforementioned philosophical debates.

It is probably worth interjecting at this point with a small word of warning: this relationship will deplete your bank account. You have been warned.

Fortunately, it is unlikely that your new best friend will

be presumptuous enough to request anything more expensive than your common or garden cooking sherry.

As your friendship progresses, the conversation may move to the subject of religion. If this happens my best advice to you would be to retreat. Whilst you, dear reader, have been languishing in front of the goggle box, your only opinions of religion derived from assembly at school and Sunday morning television viewed through the haze of a hangover, your trampy friend has been busy.

His mind has been questing. He has been honing his abilities. And not just at swilling grog. I mean, how else could he stand the boredom? Chances are your friendly neighbourhood vagrant is closer to Nietzsche than you would dare to give him credit. Most likely he is part of an underground army of nihilists ready to systematically unpick your belief system until you reach the point where, over perhaps your second or third sip of de-icer, you are ready to embrace their ways.

And then it will be time. You can shed your consumerist shell.

Vanish.

Into the undergrowth of the local park. To let your hair become matted into one long dreadlock like an otter's tail hanging down your back. To shout at passers by. To shout at imaginary hedgehogs.

To take your consciousness to the next level and finally

embrace the truth that not only have you reached the next level but that the only true meal, the only one that counts, is sherry for breakfast.

SPROUTS

THERE'S this man. He's just moved in next door. And the thing is I'm pretty sure that he has sprouts instead of eyes. Specifically brussels sprouts although I'm not sure that there are any other kind.

Of sprouts I mean, not eyes.

And this is not just some simple mistake, like thinking someone has carrots for fingers or potatoes for knees or a cauliflower-arse (long story – suffice to say people look very different through frosted glass and I don't speak to the people across the street now).

My wife thinks it's becoming an obsession, but she doesn't know the half of it. I never got around to telling her about the issue with the cauliflowers. She still thinks that when she smiles at the people from across the road and they turn away with disdain it's because she has a better car than them, better dress sense, whatever. I mean, she has, but that's not the real reason they do it. Not the *real* reason.

You see, the new neighbour was getting out of his car, this would have been a few days or maybe a week after he and his vegetable-bride moved in. He had a couple of carrier bags full of groceries, and I said hello to him because, well, I'm neighbourly like that. Ask me for a cup of sugar and I'll punch you square in the face, but a polite greeting over the fence is no problem. It's all about scale.

He mumbled something back – could have been anything. Sounded like 'Yorkshire puddings' to me. I let it pass but as he glanced up at me – by this time I'm almost in the house, opening the door, putting the keys back in my pocket – and I see a flash of green.

He has eyelids. Proper ones, not sheathes like the outside of a sprout, but human eyelids, and underneath – sprout.

I shut the door quickly but then got an overwhelming urge to see if it was true or just a trick of the light. Were my eyes playing tricks on me?

Two days later I knocked on their door. I had an excuse ready: I was waiting for a delivery, and had it been left at their house? I knocked. Waited. The door opened and it was his bride, displaying no vegetable-features whatsoever.

I used the excuse and went back into my house.

After that I began sitting at our front window with the lights out, waiting for him to come home. I was ready, coiled to spring out and look him straight in the sprouts. But I get bored easily, so ended up watching TV instead. A programme came on about an unorthodox detective and I kept imagining it was me. Except that instead of investigating the brutal stabbing of a middle-aged man I was investigating…

Well, I was investigating sprouts. There was no other way of dressing it up.

The problem was that after a couple of weeks I found myself watching TV daytime, evening, and night-time, and my investigation ground to a halt. I found myself investigating TV much more successfully. I did what any unorthodox detective would do when presented with a situation such as this – I gave up. My wife had already convinced me that the sprouts were all in my mind, and I'd told the story to my friends so many times that it had become practised. I'd honed the details, stressed the funny parts, spun it out. It was at the stage where even I didn't believe it.

Then there was a knock on the door. I opened it and there stood Mrs Cauliflower from across the road. I balked slightly then snapped on a smile.

'How are you? What can I do for you?'

'You're vegetable obsessed aren't you?' she asked.

'I wouldn't go that far, I mean it was a misunderstanding that's all.' I moved the door closed ever so slightly.

'It's just that you know that man? The one who lives there?' she pointed to the house next door.

I nodded.

'I think he might have sprouts for eyes.'

RUDOLPH REDUX

SOON after what I now refer to as my 'Holiday Incident', I started writing '*Happy Holidays?*' in cards instead of '*Merry Christmas!*'

My wife was screaming out of the landing window.

'You are not putting that monstrosity on *my* roof.'

I looked down at Rudolph, standing two feet tall next to me. His paint was peeling, and one antler had broken off, leaving only a long, sharp, shard pointing straight up. A long length of cable protruded from his worn posterior. When plugged in, it would illuminate him for the whole neighbourhood to see.

Of course that wasn't the thought going through my head as I hung from the roof of my house. The electrical cord wrapped around my foot was the only thing keeping me from falling two stories and landing on my head. And Rudolph? Well, instead of lighting up, he was swinging and repeatedly smashing into my face. My wife was inside the house, and I was shouting, and maybe I was screaming. When I eventually told the story to my friends I didn't mention the screaming.

I could see frost on the garden as I spun above it, twisting in the air, being attacked by a shabby reindeer.

'What do you want? I'm trying to get ready. We're going out in half an hour.'

I could hear her through the bedroom window. She sounded the same upside down as she did the right way up.

Dear Santa, I have been a very good boy this year, please don't let me become the person they remember as Reindeer Man.

LOCAL MAN FOUND WITH HEAD UP REINDEER'S ARSE.

Children would make pilgrimages to the place where Rudolph nearly bought the big one.

'No, darling. Santa was worried, but it was alright in the end – Rudolph could fly but the Reindeer Man couldn't.'

I kept thinking of ice skaters and how they keep their balance after spinning around over and over. My memory was telling me that they tried to keep focussed on one fixed point, so I tried it, and the number on door 81 became my focus. Really I was just trying to keep from thinking about how old the cable was and how it would snap at any second.

I started in the loft looking for decorations, except I was fairly sure we didn't have any because we'd just moved into the house two months ago. My wife was at the bottom of the ladder saying, 'Just go to the shop and buy a tree. If you wait for five minutes I'll come with you and help you choose baubles.'

Notice the careful positioning of the word 'help'.

So, of course, I ignored her and started rummaging, a medium-sized torch shoved into my mouth, wedging it so far open that my jaw ached and saliva ran down at the corners. It was a treasure trove up there, but for every box I opened, for every neatly wrapped nugget of a forgotten holiday season I found, I was greeted with a thump, a bump, or a grump from the Grinch downstairs.

Dear Santa, although I have not been a particularly good boy this year I was wondering whether you would see your way clear to leaving me a ball gag and restraints. They aren't for me, so I thought you may make an exception.

It was then I found him. My soon-to-be nemesis. Dusty. Forgotten. Rudolph.

I struggled to carry him down the ladder to the landing,

put him lightly on the ground, and began dusting him off. It elicited exactly the response I expected.

'What the bloody hell is that?' screamed my current nemesis.

On the third day of Christmas my true love gave to me; three blazing rows, two dirty looks, and a promise there'd be no sex for me.

There were these carol singers in Australia who had gone out to do their thing and two of them had died of sunstroke. Perfectly normal thing to do at that time of year, but they got carried away, filled with the spirit of the season and that was it, game over.

Rudolph was heavy, and it took me some time to wrestle the damn thing step by step, hauling it towards its appointment on the roof. By the time we reached our destination, I was panting from the effort. I put him down by my side and bent over, my hands on my knees as I tried to catch my breath and... well you know the rest.

Dear Santa, thank you for the lovely flowers. And the grapes. The doctors and nurses have been wonderful and, although the injuries I suffered were extensive, only one of them is permanent. As I fell, the only thing that stopped my face from hitting the pavement was a certain red-nosed friend of yours. I have been in touch with my lawyer who says I have a good case against you as I was erecting an effigy in your honour. You will be hearing from us in due course.

A long time later, many months after I got out of the hospital, my wife and I returned to the old house. It was early December. I'd grown used to wearing the patch over my eye. We stood, the cold biting at us, my arm around her as she snuggled in for warmth and we looked at the house.

After a couple of minutes my wife said, 'Come on darling, it's freezing. Can we go now?'

I smiled and nodded, kissed her brow and a kid ran out of the open garage wrapped up and ready for the cold. He ran past us, did a double take and stopped.

'Mister,' he said, staring at me wide-eyed. 'Are you a pirate?'

I laughed and shook my head.

'Wh-?' he began but the sentence stalled.

'You have to be a good boy at Christmas time,' I said, leaning in close to impart secret knowledge to him. 'I was a bad boy and Rudolph did this to me with his antlers...'

I lifted the patch. The kid screamed and ran. To destroy the good name of Rudolph was one of the things I enjoyed most.

My wife and I turned our backs on the incident at number 18 and went to find a bar we used to drink in.

SPECIAL K AND THE YORKSHIRE TERRIER

I FELT a lot more comfortable with robbing the vet this time. The idea itself had been in my mind for, I don't know, maybe twelve months, and as I sat in the waiting area I knew I'd nailed it.

I'll admit it, the first time, I tried was a shambles. I assumed too much, indeed I consumed too much. Fact: whiskey steadies your nerves. By the time my nerves were steady enough I was so pissed I couldn't find the place.

The last time I tried it I lost my nerve, threw in the towel before the bell rang to start the fight, but I'd made my mistakes, learned my lessons.

So there I sat in full withdrawal, the bags under my eyes trailing so low it felt like they were touching the tops of my shaking hands. Trudy didn't mind, she just panted, and relished what she thought to be the attention I was giving her.

I should probably mention that Trudy was my decoy on this mission. She was my brother's Yorkshire terrier, and a fine decoy she had so far proved to be.

The nurse finally called my name, and I moved towards her.

Fact: this wasn't my real name, but a pseudonym.

To use your real name in a situation like this would be truly idiotic.

Inside the vet's inner sanctum I placed Trudy on the operating table and took a step back, keeping her leash tight in my hand. The breeze from the closing door blew cold across the clammy nape of my neck.

'So what can we do for you today then?' asked the vet with a smile.

I drew the heavy weight of the .45 from my jacket and levelled it at his head.

'You can put your hands in the air for a start,' I said and swallowed, my throat dry.

'Sit,' I said, waving the gun towards a solitary metal chair.

The vet and Trudy did as they were told in unison.

'Now stay,' I added. The vet didn't move. Trudy yapped.

A second later the nurse returned to the room, but I was ready for her.

'Not a sound,' I hissed. 'Shhh! This will be over very quickly.' Trudy yapped again.

The nurse nodded behind scared eyes. I could feel myself panting over my parched tongue, the gun too heavy and desperately cold in my hand.

'Where,' I asked, 'do you keep the ketamine?'

'We – um – don't have any?' said the vet. 'We are waiting for – erm – that is, an order that was – um – Monday! I was operating on a horse, you see and we, that is, I used all of our stock sedating it. It's not due until Monday.'

I tried to stay calm. Had I blown it? Trudy began yapping repeatedly, high pitched, piercing and insistent. I felt a tic developing in my left temple.

'Shut up,' I screamed.

Trudy whimpered.

I grabbed the nurse and looked at the vet. 'Do you want to have to hire a new assistant?'

'I – I – er,' the vet began.

The nurse coughed and pointed at a fridge on the far wall. I let her go and pulled Trudy's lead. She hopped to the ground and trotted over with me.

It was a dirty business, I reasoned as I drove away. I had managed to get a rucksack full of horse tranquillisers.

Maybe my luck was turning. And my brother told me no one ever robs vets.

That's the point, I told him. That's the point.

A STROLL ALONG THE PROM, PROM, PROM

THE promenade had long ago begun to disintegrate and the council's lack of interest meant that no-one even walked down the prom the way they used to.

Two elderly gentlemen moved stoically along, lost in a world where the prom was freshly painted and it wasn't a dangerous place to be.

'You seen Dave at the club then?' asked Mac, his cane not really making much contact with the ground.

'Nah, Tommy said he was on his last legs at the home,' replied Percy.

'Bastard still owes me a tenner.'

'You'll never see that again.'

'Remember when he lost that bet with the sergeant and

didn't have any money?'

Percy laughed, 'Yes, and the Sarge beat him to within an inch of his life!'

The pair stopped by one of the booths that peppered the prom and stared out to sea, both lost in the memory.

Out of the shadows of a viewing booth a teenager stepped into their path. They stopped.

'Money. And your watches. Now, Granddads!' the kid screamed, spittle flying from his mouth. He shoved the stickless Percy backwards.

Carefully, the old man reached into his coat pocket and rummaged for something.

Meanwhile Mac lifted his cane into the air, whirling it around and connecting with the kid's temple with a crunch.

The teenager crumpled to the ground, and Percy pulled his hand from his pocket and the blade of a knife jumped out to slice through the sea-fretted air. Percy lunged forward towards the prone kid lying face-down on the ground and slid the knife into his back under the ribs.

A hiss escaped from between the kid's lips and he fell forward to the floor, his hands grasping out for anything, his jaw opening and closing like a fish's dragged from the sea. Percy lowered himself carefully to the boy's side, and gently placed his leather-gloved hand over the boy's mouth and nose, and watched as he slowly, silently suffocated.

'Lung?' asked Mac.

'Lung,' Percy nodded.

The kid's mouth was still bobbing as his face began to turn blue.

The pair moved off a little faster than before.

'Where'd you learn that?' asked Mac. 'The Sarge?'

A smile cracked across Percy's face as the memory played back in his mind.

SANDWICHES

DAVE is sitting on a bench in a shopping mall between two old people. He is thinking about sandwiches. He has been there for over an hour and is undis-
turbed by the presence of the old lady to his right (smelling
overpowering of lavender) and the old man to his left
(smelling faintly of wee). Beads of sweat have formed on
his brow as he thinks, as hard as he has ever thought on any
subject, about sandwiches.

What is the best sandwich I have ever eaten? How can
he possibly gauge this? Surely, he wonders as he becomes
more and more worried, it must be there, hidden in his
mind. His eyes flicker up top-right; he is trying to remember, trying to catch the memory wherever it is hidden but

he cannot find it.

He rubs his leg, trying to keep it from pins and needles and mentally probes further. It may not be the best sandwich ever made. No. But the best sandwich he personally has ever tasted. He fidgets because he knows it is something he should know.

He knows what his favourite film is. It is *Every Which Way But Loose* because he loves Clint Eastwood and he loves monkeys. It combines both flawlessly and therefore it is his favourite film. Every other film he has ever watched could be compared to it and graded accordingly. In the unlikely event that a better film is ever made, then the whole grading system will have to be mentally adjusted to accommodate.

But he just couldn't apply a grading system to sandwiches.

There was a steak sandwich he remembered eating some three years previously. The waitress in the restaurant had asked him how he wanted the steak. He chose rare, and the sandwich had a dressing that complemented the meat perfectly. But indecision is rife. He is not certain that this is the best sandwich he has ever tasted.

One thing Dave is sure about is that he can rule out any sandwich he has made himself, as his own sandwiches never seem to turn out as well as those that are prepared by others.

The old woman turns to look at him and stares in a way that demands he turn and address her. He resists. And decides to buy a notebook so that he might chronicle every sandwich he eats from that moment on.

He rises to his feet and walks on from the bench, safe in the knowledge that, once again, his life has order.

SELF ASSEMBLY

'WHERE'S the painting? The canvas, Clint – where is it?'

Big Terry pushed the gun into Clint's temple, forcing him down to the ground, his face pressed against cardboard packaging. Clint inhaled sharply and cardboard fibres rushed into his lungs. For once he wished for sleep. This time it didn't come. Apparently the drugs did work. Bugger.

'I favour the Tate Modern myself,' said Big Terry, continuing an already established monologue. 'Last time I was in London I went in there and it was inspiring. Not that I understand all of it, mind you. And I don't think they put much thought into people like me coming along when they hang the paintings. Well why would they?'

'I'm not sure,' said Clint.

Big Terry stood over Clint, staring at him with little beads of sweat starting to form above his thick, black eyebrows.

'That was a rhetorical question,' he said. 'When I want an answer from you, it will be preceded by a sudden feeling of pain, do you understand?'

Big Terry carefully stood on Clint's hand, he yelped and twisted to try to extricate himself.

'Yesyesyes. Yes I understand. Jesus, this is nothing to do with me I keep telling you.'

Big Terry began walking away, looking for something.

'You can open the box now.'

Clint did as he was instructed and began to try to tear his way into whatever this flat-pack furniture Big Terry had forced him to drag out here. Of course he had been contemplating its contents ever since Big Terry turned up at his home.

It hadn't taken him long, one of his goons had kicked the door in. Clint heard Big Terry's voice then... he woke up in the boot of a car. By the time they stopped driving and opened the boot he had a very good idea what was in the box he had been lying on, however he wasn't about to admit that to himself let alone Big Terry. The cardboard quickly gave way, revealing some neatly packed pieces of wood, a plastic bag full of metal fixings and a sheet of instructions. Clint looked at them for a moment before climbing back to his feet.

'You want me to build you a desk out here?' he asked without thinking, instantly regretting it.

Big Terry stopped dead. His hand gripped the gun tighter and he turned back to face Clint, squinting in the evening sun and casting a surprisingly long shadow on the forest floor.

'Is that it?' He knew if he had made a mistake it was too late to do anything about it and instinctively went with it. 'You threaten me, you kidnap me, you drag me out here to the middle of nowhere in a blindfold, make me drag this shit all the way out here and then you want me to make you a fucking desk? Or perhaps I'm wrong, perhaps it's a nice shelving unit.'

Big Terry raised his arm and squeezed a single shot at Clint, the bullet burying itself in the tree behind him.

'I suggest you shut the fuck up and read the instructions. Now, I'm busy. I'm looking for something. I'll be around. Watching. Get building, dipshit.' He moved off into the woods out of Clint's line of sight.

Clint stared for a moment at the space Big Terry had occupied. He should make a run for it. But what was the point? Where would he go? Big Terry had picked him up at his own house, he knew about Katie and to be brutally honest he didn't really have a clue as to how to get back to wherever the hell the car was anyway. It seemed that for now furniture assembly was on the cards.

He removed the pieces of wood one by one and laid them out on the soil around him; six pieces of wood in three pairs. He knew what it was. Two of the pairs were similar, over six feet long but one pair thinner than the other. The final pair were two small squares. As he knelt down to arrange the pieces on the ground pine needles stuck sharply into his flesh.

Shelves, he thought. Perhaps Big Terry has befriended a fox in need of storage solutions.

Clint picked up the bag of fixings and tossed it from hand to hand. Carefully, he pierced the plastic with his fingers and poured out the contents onto one of the pieces of wood. He reached out a hand a spread them before finally picking up and unfolding the instructions. He looked at the list of items that should be included and stared for a second.

Two small square bits of wood. Check

Two long slim bits of wood. Check.

Two long wider bits of wood. Check.

Twenty-eight nails.

He began counting but only reached twenty-four before he ran out. Damn it. He started again, this time he had only twenty-three nails. Either way there weren't enough.

'Bi-' he began but thought better of it. Most likely Big Terry would do something unspeakable if he found out. He decided the best course of action was to do the same thing he did at home – bodge the job.

He looked back to the list and that was it. Wasn't it? He moved his index finger downwards, his lips moving as he read again.

Yes, that was it. He needed a hammer but he wasn't going to ask Big Terry for that. That was a sure fire way to get the claws lodged in the back of his head.

'You want a hammer, I'll give you a hammer,' Clint muttered under his breath, surveying the scene around him for a rock or something heavy enough to knock the nails in with. As he did so he turned over the paper in his hands to see the instructions for building the thing. His eyes widened as he stared at the page but before he could really take in what he was seeing the wind blew, catching the instructions and whipping them into the air.

'Shit!' he screamed, the air rushing from his lungs. The same voice bounced back at him from the surrounding trees after he leapt towards the instructions. Spitting guttural obscenities he hunted down the instructions, finally grabbing them once more as they caught on a small branch that he kicked at until it splintered. His tantrum over, he turned and walked calmly back towards the waiting wood, reading as he went.

The instructions were the kinds that are designed for anyone of any nationality to understand. Pictures carefully illustrated each stage of construction, four of them in total. The first picture portrayed a smiling red man standing over one of the long, wide pieces of wood that obviously served as a base for the box. He waited, hammer in hand as his smiling green friend held the two long thin pieces of wood in place.

The second picture showed the two friends nailing the end pieces in place to form a long, thin box. The red man didn't look as happy in this picture for reasons that were all too apparent.

Picture three showed the red man lying in the box while the green man nailed him in and picture four showed a section view of the red man at the bottom of a grave, nailed into his coffin and apparently banging on the lid of the casket he had just helped to build. Mr. Green stood above ground where the sun shone with a spade in one hand and a hammer in the other. Clint thought the bastard looked smug.

With a gait like a drum roll, Big Terry came scuttling out of the woods behind Clint. He spun round on the log he was perched upon but wasn't quick enough. Big Terry brought the butt of his pistol into sharp contact with Clint's temple. Clint crumpled to the ground and Big Terry stood over him, one foot either side of his head as he stared down at the blood trickling from the wound he had inflicted.

'I thought I told you not to try to escape?' he said. 'It's understandable I suppose, once you unpacked the surprise… I found what I was looking for by the way.'

'Oh good,' said Clint, trying unsuccessfully to reach up to his forehead to check his injury.

'Yes, I asked a friend of mine to come out here and dig me a big hole. Just big enough to fit that lovely box in and amazingly it is six feet deep.'

Clint raised an eyebrow; he could feel blood starting to trickle from his brow to his hairline.

'Yes, well that's why I asked him to do it isn't it?' Big Terry snapped. 'Anyway that's not the point! How did you like my instructions?'

Clint stared at Big Terry for a moment, his breathing shallow.

'Oh, this time you can speak – I really am interested to know. I designed them myself you know.'

'They blew away in the wind,' said Clint, determined not to let Big Terry know how much this really was beginning to get to him. He was pretty sure his voice only cracked once.

'I know – I saw but you read them, right?'

'Yes. I read them.'

'And?' said Big Terry, fidgeting with his gun.

'And I'm glad it's not shelving. I'm fucking hopeless at

putting up shelving.'

Big Terry raised his right foot and placed it squarely on Clint's nose, exerting just the tiniest amount of pressure.

'Now Clint,' he began. 'I know you're a cocky little bastard but we can play this one of two ways. Either you can tell me what I want to know…'

Clint could smell the fresh soil between the treads on Big Terry's shoes. He tried unsuccessfully to turn his head as Big Terry began to put pressure on his face.

'Or I can and will bury you alive out here and you can starve to death in your own personal hell six feet under the ground. How does that sound?'

'Mmmmmmph,' replied Clint.

'I'll tell you what. Why don't you get going with the carpentry and you can decide in a few minutes.' Big Terry took his foot from Clint's face before kicking him in the ear.

'Ow!' Clint screamed, scrambling out of the way. 'That hurt.'

'No shit,' said Big Terry and began moving back towards the flat pack. 'Now come on, start hammering.'

A few minutes later and Clint was hammering only a few feet away from the gaping hole Big Terry had discovered.

'Terry,' said Clint.

'Big Terry.'

'Sorry, um, Big Terry. I shouldn't be here you know.'

'Oh shouldn't you? And why is that exactly?'

'I was only ever a messenger. I don't have the painting.'

'Don't play the innocent with me you little shit – you've ripped me off one too many times *boy*.'

'Wh-'

'Anyway, shut up. Are you nearly finished?'

Clint stood over the coffin he had constructed. The wood was rough and unvarnished.

'Listen,' said Clint. 'About that painting…'

He knew his only chance was to convince Big Terry that he really didn't know where the damn thing was but even with the pleading tone he had inadvertently adopted Big Terry remained ice cold.

'Ah yes, now we get to it.'

'I really don't know where it is,' said Clint, deflated by the response.

Big Terry stared at Clint unblinking.

'Listen, Big Terry…'

Big Terry took the pistol from his coat and cocked the hammer.

'This can't be happening, you've got to be kidding.'

He waved the pistol at Clint, who shook his head.

'No, I'm not getting into that fucking box.'

'Yes you are.'

Clint had begun to sweat. Not the healthy, wholesome sweat of DIY but a cold, creeping sweat that began in the small of his back and had begun working its way outwards.

'I'm really not. This… this… it's not…' Clint waved his hands in front of him and took a step back.

Big Terry got up from where he was sitting and walked across to Clint, smiling a friendly smile.

'Now Clint, earlier on I gave you a choice. I appreciate that you maintain you do not know anything about the painting. For now, I am prepared to believe you.'

'Thank God! Oh, Big Terry, I won't forget this I was really starting to panic about that whole being buried alive deal.'

Big Terry shook his head and held the barrel of his gun in front of his lips like an index finger. 'Shhhh. Earlier I gave you a choice and the choice was you either tell me where the painting is or you will be buried alive.'

Clint nodded.

'Unfortunately I don't feel I can renege on that offer and I am going to have to bury you alive.'

Clint wondered if it would make any difference if he threw up on Big Terry. He swallowed the foul gastric taste that had suddenly pervaded his palette.

'However as you didn't have the opportunity to save yourself I am going to give you a second choice.'

'Wh-?'

'I can shoot you.'

Clint stared at Big Terry as he lifted the gun and pointed it at him.

'Or not.' Big Terry raised his empty left hand and made his thumb and index finger into the shape of a gun before pulling the imaginary trigger and winking his eye.

Big Terry began to blur in front of Clint's eyes. He lifted his hand and touched his face, tears streamed down. There was nothing else he could do; he could practically feel the consciousness slipping away from him. Clint began sobbing.

'Is this dignified? Clint? Is it?' Big Terry shook his head.

'Well?'

Clint sobbed.

'I'm sorry but we really are going to have to wrap things up. I need your final answer.'

Clint shook his head.

'Okay then. In the box.'

Clint looked first at the box, then at the hole in the ground and, like the red man, got inside and lay down. The tears rolled down his cheeks and onto the untreated wood beneath. A splinter was sticking in his thigh but he didn't move. There was no point.

Moments later Big Terry poked his head into view. 'Actually, can you just get out for a second?'

Clint did as he was told, his eyes fixed on the gun the whole time.

'Tall aren't you?' Big Terry grabbed the coffin and dragged it to the edge of the grave.

'I don't mean to be.'

'You can pop back in now, I just thought it'll be easier to tip you in from there.'

Clint repeated instruction number three and waited for the green man to follow through with his instructions.

Soon the lid of the coffin was in place. Big Terry, although muted, still continued talking outside.

'It's probably the best choice if I'm honest,' he said. 'If nothing else it proves you have hope.'

With each nail that was hammered in, Clint felt the vibrations through the wood, the sound echoed in his ears and the tears kept rolling down his face. He had stopped sobbing now and just stared at a spot two inches in front of his face, the claustrophobia starting to take hold.

'I mean you never know, you may be rescued.'

He had been counting the nails and he knew that there had already been twenty-two used. That left one or two and then that would be it.

'Not that any humans come out this far into the woods. Perhaps a passing fox will hear your cries and call his friends together to dig you up.'

With one last bang nail number twenty-four reached its

destination.

'It'll be like *Wind in the Willows*.'

Clint lay for a second trying to think of something to do, a plan, anything. Nothing came. He could feel the coffin tilting and after a moment it dropped, hitting the bottom of the grave, knocking the wind out of him and winking out the light of his consciousness. He passed out.

IS THAT TO GO?

GEOFF and Martin are sitting in a popular global coffee outlet which I shouldn't name for legal reasons (it's Starbucks). They have been there for some time and Geoff has become concerned.

'Martin,' Geoff begins, on the verge of reiterating what the author just pointed out. 'I'm worried about you.'

Martin shakes his head rapidly left and right.

Geoff sips his coffee. It tastes great: not too warm, not too cold, not too strong, not too weak. Fan-bloody-tastic.

Martin continues to shake his head leftright.

Geoff reaches out and places his mug on the table between them, then gently extends his palm and places it on Martin's juddering forearm. Martin stops momentarily, his gaze crunching to a halt on the back of Geoff's hand.

'How much coffee have you had?' But Geoff already knows the answer.

'No-noNOtenOugh. Not. No. Notenough. Enough. No. Nono.'

Geoff stares at Martin like a long lost lover, wondering where it all went wrong. But Geoff knows. Martin was holidaying in the US and saw a TV report about McDonald's being sued over the temperature of their coffee. Easy, he thought as he returned on the plane. Some minor oral scalding, and I can retire early.

Martin had not counted on the McDonald's communication system working faster than a bush telegraph, faster even than a 747, and it wasn't until he reached Casualty that he realised a warning message had been placed on the cup.

Unperturbed, he had looked for his own niche. His own way of fucking the corporate world over. Geoff had a funny feeling that Martin had found the niche.

'Five hours,' Martin begins cautiously, his eyes fizzing with static, darting up-up-down. 'FifteenNnNoNONine-TEEN.'

Geoff makes to interrupt but Martin jitters beyond interjection, throwing Geoff's palm from his arm with a shout.

'Yesteen. Nineteen. Nineteen CofFees. Nine. Teen.'

His head drops to the table and his arms snap over the top. 'STOP!'

For the time it takes to slice the cheesecake there is silence then he's whipped upright and scratching at his forearm, scratching like someone had slipped a leech under there and it was slowly sucking the life blood from him.

'McMc' he purses his lips, staring at Geoff.

'Donald's?'

'Right! Donald's. Didn't work. No, nope no way not that one, didn't go to plan. This one will it will it will. YesyesYES.'

Martin nods and nods updownupdownupdown.

'Martin,' asks Geoff between the virtual seizures before him. 'What are you...'

'Doing? GoodquestionknewYOUwouldask. Brightman, cleverbloke. In. The. Know.' He draws breath then: 'TwentytwentySIX coffees. Twintowntwentysixsexsixy six SIX. Twentysix and that's the strike. No warning nowarning body cantake it. Can't handle it nowaynohow. No. No. Get to twenty SIX! Twentysixthecharm then downdowndown.'

He stops mid-yammer to jab a sweaty finger at his cup.

'No warning,' he hisses, as he leans forward as if pushing all his concentration into his frontal lobes. 'Twenty Seven. Cups. Grande. Will. Kill. ThenweSUE. Lawyers. MmmmHmm.'

Geoff stands up and ruffles his friend's hair playfully. 'Martin?'

'Yes. YES!'

Geoff clenches his fist and punches Martin as hard as he can square in the face.

DIAL M FOR MONKEY

IT HAPPENS

TWO *bottles of wine. Red. Australian Merlot. Chinese microwave food. Chow Mein. With chicken – chewy. Television all evening. American sitcoms. Funnier the more wine I drink. She arrives then... Cold porcelain against my cheek as I recover from emptying the evening's entertainment into the toilet. Brief relief.*

The soft duvet wrapped around me, protecting me from the world spinning around and then instant, complete unconsciousness. At last.

'Okay, okay. I got that part,' said the sergeant, leaning across the table in the interview room. 'But what else happened?'

I wake up to the cat licking my face. By the time I pull

my eyes open I realise something is wrong. It happens. I rush to the toilet and know it happened again last night. The duvet spills out behind me like the cape of some drunken super-hero and I go, pissing sitting down, head in hands, elbows on my knees as I sit, my world tilting and rutting. I return to the bedroom to see her lying there. Silent.

The sergeant leant back in his chair. This was the fourth time he had heard the story. He rubbed his forehead with grimy fingers and nodded slightly.

'Go on.'

I stumble towards my dressing gown and somehow manage to get my arms through the right holes. I don't worry about covering myself up, I know there's no point. For a second I think I might need to run back to the toilet but it passes.

I walk slowly over to her. She is lying face down, one hand above her head, one behind her back which I notice is smooth and unblemished. I extend a shaky finger and lightly jab her buttock a couple of times. Just to see. Nothing.

'Good,' the sergeant said. 'This is better but how did she get there?'

There was a pause before the suspect continued.

She must have used the key I gave her to get into the house. I have this arrangement with her, whenever I go away on business, on holiday, whatever, she comes and feeds my cat. It's very kind, she doesn't have to. In return I do this for her. It isn't a spoken agreement, just something that has evolved over the ten years we've been neighbours.

'So she was your neighbour?' he said. Somewhere in this blank exterior there may be an explanation.

It's very remote where we live. There are just two houses set back from the beach, side by side. We're never disturbed. Not another house for miles. The majority of the time it's the epitome of coastal living but sometimes when the darkness comes I get jumpy.

'Jumpy? What do you mean jumpy? When my wife walks about at night she gets jumpy, she doesn't go around killing people – d'you see?'

Being here in the country should mean I can leave my doors unlocked and sleep easy. Maybe because I live on my own I don't necessarily see the good in everyone as easily as I should. Call it survival instinct.

So there she was, in the bed. My bed. This woman, this invader, this uninvited guest. I grab her and hoist her over onto her back. She's a dead weight.

The sergeant sighed and tapped his pen on the desk. None of this was fitting together the way he had hoped.

I can't think of her sexually, not any more. Not after what has happened. I try to make sure my eyes don't spend too long on any part of her body. It turns my stomach to think of it now. I lay her arms by her sides and go to begin preparations. Her lipstick is long-faded, her lips giving way to a blue tinge around the edges. My eyes glance for a second to her neck. It's a bullet wound this time. The downy hair on the nape is scorched. The gun would have been fired at close range. It happens.

'Hang on,' he blurted. 'What do you mean "it happens"? So someone came in when you were drunk and shot her?' He moved forward so he was eye to eye with the suspect and shot him his best intimidating glare.

I think about her as I dig in the sand outside. I wonder what sort of woman she had been as I bundle her into the wheelbarrow. As I drop her into the shallow grave half a mile from the house I wonder what it would have sounded like when she laughed.

He felt a sinking feeling in his stomach, a mixture of adrenaline and sadness. He knew what was coming next.

I never cover the graves. Not until weeks afterward. It isn't like anyone would ever come out here and, besides, the seagulls will soon begin their pecking, the predators will visit tonight, the wildlife will do what they do. It's easy enough to come back later and bury what's left of the evidence. Nature is very effective.

The sergeant glanced from the suspect to the tape recording the interview. Just to make sure. One time he had forgotten to record a confession. It happens.

At least the cat will be fed, I think to myself as I wander back home.

The following day the sergeant arrived at the suspect's house. Other cars would be there soon but he wanted to be there first, to see. The car door clunked shut and his attention was caught by a cat scampering towards him. The tabby jumped onto the bonnet of his car, desperate for affection and probably for food. He stroked it for a second and noticed its healthy coat, its bright new collar.

He looked up at the house in front of him and took his notebook out of his shirt pocket, flipping it open as he did so. He read carefully and was about to make his way inside when he noticed the house stood alone.

No neighbour. No house next door. It complicated matters. It happens.

TO LET: GROUND FLOOR FLAT

THEY'VE been living in the upstairs flat for six months.

He: fashionable, hair by Toni & Guy, music taste the worst side of Radio 1's playlist, king of take-aways, would never be seen in a bar that served real ale.

She: heart-shaped face, beautiful big eyes, dresses like an explosion on the catwalk, hair also by Toni & Guy, music taste unknown but certainly turns down the pop-crud of He, can almost certainly never touch his take-aways judging by her hourglass figure, and for God's sake don't get me started on her arse...

I see them coming and going, see She sweeping in and storming out. And I hear them. The music, as I may have mentioned was fucking appalling.

But what was really appalling was the fucking.

He was so bad at it. She seemed to make the best of it but, to be honest, He was the worst I had ever heard. And it has to be pointed out at this stage that I was single so I was in no real position to criticise. However, single or not, everyone knows bad fucking when you hear it.

The shared garden – that was my undoing.

He: out for the day, hadn't seen him for hours.

She: outside in a bikini looking like a curtain twitcher's wet dream. Which was handy as that was exactly what this curtain twitcher was looking for.

Two hours of foreplay followed with She slowly marinating in the attention. I gazed from behind the veil of muslin, struggling with the inner turmoil of whether or not it constituted an invasion of privacy if I only took photos of her on my phone.

By the time dusk came I was almost ready to do the same myself. She started to make moves towards going inside, putting her magazine to one side, stretching. When He arrived home and kissed She with a passion I thought only I had for her, I felt positively voyeuristic.

I was all set to turn to my imagination to finish what She had started in my boxers when it started. Slowly at first. The thumping rhythm of love. Right from the moment they got inside.

It was as if he'd been out all day taking lessons. The pace steadily rising thump-thump-thumping in a way that I was sure She was enjoying but had to admit I wasn't exactly finding it repulsive myself. As the thumping quickened upstairs, so my own pace quickened downstairs until it was all too much and... well, you can fill in the rest for yourself, I'm sure.

The following day a parcel was delivered while they were out and He came to collect it.

'I couldn't help overhearing you yesterday evening,' I said with a smirk, hoping to elicit embarrassment, to move myself up the playground hierarchy.

'Ah yes,' he replied without flinching. 'Sorry if I disturbed you. I was putting together an Ikea cupboard.'

My relationship with She was over and I moved out soon after, but have since been strangely drawn towards flat-packed furniture.

ADAM MAXWELL

THE DANGERS OF eBAY

ENTER YOUR WISH HERE. PLEASE BE CONCISE AND SPECIFIC.

They were simple enough instructions, most people seemed to be able to follow them.

SALE OF YOUR SOUL IS ETERNALLY BINDING.

WARNING: WISHES MAY NOT BE HONOURED.

That wasn't how it started of course – I had bought my first soul on eBay. It satisfied me for a while, the novelty value of owning someone else's immortal soul made me laugh. I felt like a better person, it was as if I was walking around draped in a spiritual blanket.

Soon after, my actions became somewhat erratic and, believing that I would be immune from eternal damnation,

I got involved in something that not only tarnished the soul I had bought but also cast a pretty dark shadow over my own. I knew I needed more protection and so hit upon the idea of setting up my own website. It was a simple enough affair where people could come along, fill in their name, address, email address, and check a box to say they wished to give me their immortal soul for perpetuity. So that they felt I offered a better deal than other sites of a similar nature I put in a clause by which they could retain their soul until their death, whereupon the soul would revert to me. What they got in return was whatever they wished for. In theory.

People came, of course. First tens, then hundreds, then thousands every day. Not all of them sold their soul, but many did, and I soon had more souls than I knew what to do with. I had become a soul broker.

I made sure I kept strict records, cataloguing and data-basing every soul I bought, and what their wish would be should I deign to grant it. Most were ridiculous: money, women, power. Occasionally they were worrying, with deeply disturbing undertones. These were my favourites. I would read them often. I felt close to them, fond of their unsettling tendencies, worried about them.

There was one I had become particularly obsessed by. Her name was Lynne, and she had wished for her life to end. Quickly. I worried for her, and I worried that she may be tarnishing the soul that was meant for me. After all, if I had nothing to live for I can think of a few pretty depraved things I would get into before I threw in the towel.

Soon I began waking in the night, my sheets soaked with sweat. Even in the daytime I heard voices warning me I had been duped. Perhaps her soul was already so tainted and stained that I was actually in a worse position by owning it. It was conceivable she had palmed it off onto an unsuspecting broker.

My worries finally peaked when, passing a newsagent I noticed a headline reporting the attempted suicide of a woman. She had jumped off a bridge and had broken most of the bones in her body. She was alive, but only just. In the newspaper she was identified as 'a woman from Finch Avenue'.

I didn't even need to check the address. I knew it was Lynne.

Within the hour I was at the hospital, at her bedside. I couldn't risk her behaviour any longer, I had to make sure that she didn't do anything else to what was very nearly my property. After all, you wouldn't buy a second hand car if you knew it didn't start, so why should I buy a soul that wasn't properly looked after. It was time to grant her wish.

I stood for a second looking at her looking at me and then told her I was the one who owned her soul.

'No, please!' she shouted. 'I've changed my mind.'

'Shhhh, Lynne, it's alright.' I said, smiling. 'I'm here to grant your wish.'

THE THINGS WE SAID TODAY

THERE were many things waltzing through Becky's mind as she wandered alone through the woods beside her house, but the main one was Sheila's statement from ten minutes ago:

'So we were at it and then it hit me, this gorgeous buttery orgasm.'

Becky had stared at Sheila in much the same way as she currently gazed at the way the trees gently undulated in front of her. It's not so much of a walk as it is a swim through a thick gelatinous mass, Becky grasping her way through each step, the pressure almost, but not quite, too much.

It wasn't that she was jealous. Becky had experienced

some of the best sex that she imagined anyone would be able to experience. Most of it with Mark but some of it with Vince. Good sex with toe-blasting orgasms that she felt no need to share with Sheila. Sheila obviously did not share this and rarely took more than one glass of wine before she was waxing lyrical about Bob's predilection for this, her fondness for that or their shared passion for the other.

Until now she had managed through the judicious consumption of copious amounts of red wine to blank out anything too bad but this – the buttery orgasm – this was revealed over brunch.

It was far too early to start drinking.

Wasn't it?

'And oral sex – how can you ever really be sure he's enjoying it?'

The words reverberated around her as if Sheila was following.

She stumbled forward on a fallen branch and stepped in a patch of mud, her white trainer sinking in so that she had to pull it out with an awful sucking feeling that reminded her too much of the conversation she had just walked away from.

'I'm never sure so I always keep my foot on his yoo-hoo. Just to make sure it's still – you know... standing tall.'

Sheila still sat, she assumed, in Becky's house, at Becky's table with that odd confused look she sometimes got. Becky could picture it; Sheila would be staring at the door, nibbling lightly on a shortbread biscuit, waiting for Becky's return to complete the story.

Becky turned around, facing the path home. She knew she had no choice and that she would have to tell her mother once and for all that she could not cope with stories of her parents screwing.

NOISE ABATEMENT

I T was inevitable this would happen. It is, after all why I'm at the window isn't it? Of course it is.

I wonder if they will ask the postman? Well, I suppose they will eventually. It's interesting, like watching an Agatha Christie play unfold.

The gate creaks, as it always does. I've asked the neighbours time and time again to oil it but they never listen, just agree that it's loud and something should definitely be done. It never is.

The noise jolts the postman, but not nearly as much as what he sees as he looks up: Mr No. 49 lying face down in his conservatory.

Not that that in itself is out of the ordinary. Quite the

opposite. I've seen Mr No. 49 drunk and asleep in that very place on an all too regular basis. Probably banished there by Mrs No. 49. The one thing that is out of the ordinary is that the conservatory is broken.

Into a million pieces.

And with one particular feature. The largest piece of conservatory is slicing Mr No. 49's head neatly in two. The postman looks up from his letters, is jolted to full consciousness, and finally vomits violently into the conifers. I can't help but smile.

I haven't been sleeping. It's starting to affect my work. When I'm in the office I can't keep my eyes open. Coffee keeps me awake, but I can't concentrate. It's been a month now, in the house, and I keep telling myself that they'll be quiet.

Tonight I'm sitting in the corner of the kitchen because it's the furthest point away from them. I've got a blanket over me, the radiator is at the far side of the room and it's less than efficient. I've been sat on this wooden chair for two hours and I've been treated to multiple karaoke renditions of *Suspicious Minds*.

Mr No. 49 doesn't have a good singing voice. Neither does Mrs No. 49, but they still belt it out. I sometimes feel that I'm caught in a trap, I can't walk out, because they keep me up nightly. It seems they have boundless enthusiasm for making noise. After a week of no sleep I now hate Elvis almost as much as I hate my neighbours. My ears are on the verge of the audio equivalent of repetitive strain injury from *Suspicious Minds*. I think it's got to the stage where I know the lyrics better than they do. In an attempt to salvage my sanity I go around and ask them if they would mind keeping the noise down. They reply that they would mind, and would *I* mind fucking off, if it was all the same to me.

I keep thinking they might be testing me, seeing how far they can push me before I crack. I feel close.

The tap is dripping in the sink and there's a faint creak as they stop. I know it'll just be to change the CD, but I try to take the opportunity and close my eyes. Colours throb and sleep takes me almost instantly for a few minutes before I bolt out of my chair to the over familiar *Uh huh huh* of Elvis once more.

I can't take it anymore so I wrap my blanket around me and run to the front door, bursting out of the house and down the path before doubling back and heading towards their door through their gate. I hammer on the front door until it snaps open and Mrs No. 49 stands in front of me with a dark look in her eyes.

'Please,' I say. 'Can you keep the noise down? It's half three in the morning.'

She leans outside of the house, inspecting the world.

'You're right,' she snaps. 'And if you ever come banging on my door at this time again I'll call the police.'

She slams the door in my face.

Later I'm sitting in my armchair dozing lightly in the temporary silence when, with a growl, I'm thrown back into consciousness.

He's drilling. DIY?

I can't take it.

I call the police and shove some cotton wool in my ears.

It doesn't work.

At work my boss warns me that if I fall asleep once more I'll face serious disciplinary action, or most likely the sack. As I close the door of my house behind me I contemplate leaving and finding a hotel but I know I can't afford it. And besides, as I drag myself up the stairs, I notice that there's no noise from next door. Perhaps they're out. Perhaps calling the police worked.

I smile and get into bed fully clothed, pulling the covers tight up around my head and slipping effortlessly into a deep sleep.

I dream of riches, pillows and cotton wool, floating in a land far away, selective deafness, and an ability to walk without moving my legs. I seem to float upwards for an infinite amount of time before a *tap-tap-tap* starts to pull me back towards the duvet-earth. Like warm marshmallow I start to sink into it and *tap-tap-tap* I start to panic, can't breathe and then, just as quickly as the tapping starts, it stops.

I wake up feeling refreshed and go about my morning ritual with a sense of relief. It would be nice to have neighbours I could invite over for coffee or ask to feed the cat, if I had one, but it wasn't to be. I feel a sense of sadness it took the police to shut them up but as I pull on my coat and walk out of the kitchen I don't regret it.

Until I step into the utility room to go out of the back door. In front of me is one of the strangest, most intimidating sights I've ever seen. The door is still there but someone has hammered hundreds of nine inch nails from the outside so it looks like a bed of nails. Whoever it was has been especially careful around the handle to ensure I've no hope of opening it. I panic slightly and stare blankly at the door before walking to the front door where exactly the same thing has happened.

At first I don't know what to do, so I go and sit on the stairs, the pattern on the carpet swirling sickening underneath me. It's him, I know it is. That is exactly why he was so quiet. To lull me into a false sense of security, and then hit me with this. I walk to the back door again, this time trying to turn the handle with a pair of tongs from the kitchen drawer. It doesn't work, so I run through to the lounge to phone the police. He'll pay for what he's done, I'll make sure of that. I lift the receiver, the plastic cold in my palm, and place the phone next to my ear.

Nothing.

No dial tone. Nothing.

I tap the receiver hopefully, but there's no contact with the outside world. I'm trapped in here.

It's all too much, so I just go and get into bed.

When I eventually get out of bed and climb through an upstairs window to phone the police from a telephone box they say they have already had complaints. From No. 49.

I tell them the truth but they don't care.

It's morning again and I don't go out. There's no point because my boss was less than understanding about yesterday's little fracas and told me I could have as much leave as I wanted. Unpaid, and don't come back. There's been a feeling rising inside me, and I can't resist it any-more, so I go out and knock on No. 49.

At first there's no reply, but after a moment I see the curtains upstairs twitch. I knock again, politely. I must resolve this, I can't be beaten.

The door opens, and they both stand in their dressing gowns, waiting expectantly.

'About the other night,' I begin.

They both nod.

'I just wondered if we could sort this out. Like adults.'

They stare blankly at me.

'Listen, you beat me fair and square. You proved that you're better than me so can we please call a truce?'

'I don't know what you mean,' a smirk blinks into existence on his face.

'Yes you do,' I'm beginning to lose my temper. These people can't be reasoned with. 'Listen, I know you hammered those nails through my door.'

'What nails?' she asks, grinning openly.

'The nails... in the night,' I can feel the anger turning to tears but I choke them back. 'I... Can't you let me sleep?'

They just grin back at me.

'I lost my job because of it.'

They both explode in fits of laughter. We both know they did it and I will not let it end this way.

'Listen,' he manages to say through the guffaws. 'It's nothing to do with us. We sleep during the day. Not our problem if you can't sleep.'

'Oh fuck off,' I say, their laughing echoing through the street as I turn tail and run back to my house, locking the door behind me.

I'm averaging three hours sleep a day. I think they take it in shifts to keep me awake. Why can't they see what they're doing to me? She goes out sometimes, but he doesn't. Ever. Sometimes people come to him and make more noise. I go walking now. To try to get some respite from it.

Tonight I'm on the hard shoulder of the motorway. I can feel the rush of wind each time a car blasts past. Its dark and their red taillights sparkle like stars as they zoom into the distance.

WHOOSH

I'm walking down the white line that separates the fast lane from the middle lane.

WHOOSH

It's windier here but as long as they stay in lane I'm safe…

WHOOSH

Unless someone is overtaking in which case they'll hit me and…

WHOOSH

I'll get some sleep but I…

WHOOSH

Really want to beat them…

WHOOSHWHOOSH

The bastards in No. 49…

WHOOSHWHOOSH

And then I realise what I have to do.

I try to buy a gun. They won't let me, so I buy a deactivated pistol from an old bloke in a junk shop. It's heavy and looks the part. I don't think I want to kill them, just teach them a lesson.

I've just seen her go out, so I know that this is my moment. There's a dull pounding of bass through the wall, music thumping from somewhere in their house. It's the perfect cover so I slip out and carefully make my way round to their back door.

It's louder here. I try the handle and, to my surprise, it turns; the door is unlocked. There's music seeping down from upstairs, just beginning to fade out as I gently squeeze the door shut behind me.

Suddenly, I'm having doubts. I shouldn't be doing this. Should I? I'm about to turn around and leave when I hear it, the insistent pitter-patter of the high-hat. He's playing it again.

I know it by heart, I can't walk out, I can feel myself falling over the edge.

Tip tipitip tipitipitipitip.

My hand tightens around the pistol.

Tip tipitip tipitipitipitip.

I know this is the right thing to do and my blood

seethes through my veins as he starts to sing…

We're caught by a tramp…

Little does he know that this will be the final rendition of a song that has plagued me for weeks.

Thank-ya… thank-ya very much…

It's time. I take my first tentative step out of the utility room and into the kitchen. It's a mess in here, I can hardly believe that people could live like this.

It's nice to see…

The melamine on the units is peeling, the bin is overflowing with take-away cartons and empty lager cans. I choke back a gagging reflex as the smell hits me, and I bolt into the hallway.

So many of you out tonight.

His voice is becoming clearer as I make my way down the threadbare carpet in the hall.

I gotta thank you for coming to the show.

And why should I believe him? All I've ever had is lies, threats and broken promises. Well, no more. I cross the landing toward the source of the din and stand for a split second outside the door.

Uh-huh huh.

We just cannot go on like this now can we baby?

And I begin. I can't face another line and for once I agree with Mr No. 49. We can't go on together.

'You're absolutely right,' I say as I swing open the

door and level the pistol at him. He stops singing but the music is so loud I can feel the bass pounding with my heart in my chest as it continues unperturbed.

He gazes for a moment, first at the gun, then gradually towards me and as he does so the frown that had splintered into life on his forehead begins to dissipate.

He begins to grin and starts advancing on me.

'So,' he says with a sneer. 'Decided to teach me a lesson then?'

I cock the hammer on the pistol and, to my amazement, he stops. His expression remains the same but a hollowness has entered behind his eyes and I know he's not quite sure whether or not I'm serious.

'I've asked you so many times,' I begin, my voice trembling, 'just to consider my feelings.'

He stares at me in disbelief and my hand begins to shake, my palms cold with sweat, making the gun feel like it could fall at any point. I know I must act fast.

'But every time all you do is play this fucking song. Louder.'

This time I begin advancing, my legs shaking as I drag them across the room, waving the gun in front of me.

'You see,' I am shouting now, tiny droplets of spit shooting from my mouth as I spit the words at him. 'It's very simple.'

I laugh, and as I do the tears that have been running

down my face trickle salty into my mouth.

'You must stop.'

I press the barrel of the pistol to his temple, a surge of adrenaline making me confident and euphoric.

'Any comments, apologies?'

He just gawks at me, a glazed look coming over his idiotic face. It's at that moment the music drops for the bridge and Mr No. 49 lunges towards me knocking the gun clean out of my hands, behind me onto the landing. I dive after it but he's just as quick off the mark and we crumple to the floor in a flailing scrum.

The gun is knocked through the banister and begins bouncing down the stairs. Mr No. 49 is after it, but I'm not going to let him win. Not now, not after all he's put me through. I vault over the banister and tackle him just as he's about to grab the gun.

This time I'm quickest, and spring onto the pistol, momentum carrying me back towards the kitchen. But Mr No. 49 is not to be beaten so easily and careers after me, knocking me and the gun into the pile of rubbish.

We both scrabble in the trash for the gun.

We come out at the same time, but to my dismay it's Mr No. 49 that has the gun – I've somehow grabbed a carrot.

I don't hesitate, and swing the carrot straight for his head making contact with a satisfying slapping noise. The carrot has obviously been in the bin for so long that it's no longer the traditional texture, and instead has the consistency of a rubber truncheon.

He comes back quickly, so I sprint back upstairs towards the thumping bass of *Suspicious Minds*. He's in hot pursuit and, as he bowls into the room, he knocks us both off our feet.

I react quickly, rolling to straddle him, and slapping him with the carrot. He thinks he has the upper hand as he cocks the pistol and points it at my chest.

But I know what will happen, and just keeping beating away with my orange, foot long, weapon of mass destruction. He pulls the trigger.

Nothing happens.

I hit him again, and he's bleeding, the carrot doing more damage than I thought possible.

He pulls the trigger again. Nothing. Again. Again. Again.

I don't quite know what to do next. I stop hitting him. He seems as deflated as me, and I get up, my back pressed against the window.

Then, as if electroshocked into action, he lunges up at me, hurling his whole weight through the air. But he misjudges, and hits the window, shattering it, before dropping out of sight. I spin around and look down just in time to catch the look on his face as he falls through his conservatory, demolishing it into the darkness beneath.

THE COCK AIN'T GONNA LIKE THAT

IT was only when the removal van arrived we realised we had sold our house to a truckload of chickens. Note – not a shedload. There were far more than that. There was no indication of where they had come from, there was no lower chain involved in the sale of our house, and the driver of their van was not forthcoming with the info.

It wasn't so much the conversation that was odd – their diction was perfect, the enunciation without an equal – it was more that there were over two hundred of them and they all spoke simultaneously.

'Are you leaving the curtains?' they chorused.

I wasn't, so I skirted around the question, which wasn't easy when looking straight down the beak of that many of them.

'And the kitchen appliances?' they squawked as one. 'The solicitor said that you would be leaving the white goods.'

Some of the chickens on the left side of the van had started to become restless, flapping their wings, causing one or two of them to rise into the air slightly. They didn't miss a beat though, carefully keeping exactly in time with their sisters.

'Can we come in?'

They weren't the sorts of chickens who needed an answer, and hit me like a poultry tidal wave. I staggered backwards, desperately fighting the urge to slap them back, instead keeping my hands occupied by scratching every last inch of my feather-tormented body.

'Yes,' I wheezed and dragged myself inside after them.

Inside I caught a glimpse of the last few of them heading down the hall towards the dining room and the kitchen. Against the advice of my ever-tightening lungs I followed them.

'Bok-BWARK! This fridge,' they boomed. 'How many eggs does it hold?'

I knew deep down inside that I should tell them the truth but I was relying on the fact that none of the little blighters had opposable thumbs.

'I dunno,' I panted. 'I never really counted. A lot, I

know that.'

Their little heads bobbed up and down in happy agreement.

Then there was a scratching at the door. It was the cock.

ABOUT THE AUTHOR

ADAM Maxwell was born in 1976 and has written for a plethora of publications, including Dave Eggers' *McSweeney's*, and *Tonto Short Stories*. According to his wife, he has an 'unhealthy obsession' with Bob Dylan and the Beatles, and manages to be 'increasingly worrying' in a number of other areas. He has a Masters Degree in Creative Writing from Northumbria University, and lives in the wilds of Northumberland. This is his first book. He has a website at www.adammaxwell.com.

ABOUT TONTO PRESS

TONTO Press is an independent publishing concern based in the North East of England. Formed in 2005 by authors Paul Brown and Stuart Wheatman, Tonto offers new writers more opportunities and a fair deal.

Tonto Press is named after the sidekick of the Lone Ranger, the popular Western character. Tonto was the son of a chief in the Potawatomi nation, and his name translates as 'Wild One' in his own language. He was famously portrayed on television by Jay Silverheels.

For further information about Tonto Press and our projects please visit the website www.tontopress.com.

ALSO FEATURING ADAM MAXWELL:

TONTO SHORT STORIES

Edited by Paul Brown and Stuart Wheatman

Tonto Press 2006, ISBN 0955218306, 224 pp, £9.99

Available from www.tontopress.com

and all good bookstores

TONTO Press launched its search for new writing talent with the Tonto Short Stories anthology of twenty fresh stories by twenty exciting writers. Eclectic, absorbing, affecting, and memorable, this page-turning collection represents the very best of short but sweet original fiction.

Featured stories: Stephen Shieber - The Good Little Wife; Jolene Hui - Bookshelves; Sam Jackson - Dilemma; Robin

Marsden - Nine Lies; Fiona Case - The Jellyfish; Phil Jell - Elastic Belt; Paul Brown - The Luger; Sam Morris - The Curious Anatomy of Brother Winton; Bernard Landreth - The Slug; Adam Maxwell - Self Assembly; Stuart Wheatman - Life; Dave Watson - Flux; Luke Watson - God; Eliza Hemingway - Jungle Tea; Nick Montgomery - The Last Smoker; Kirsten Bergen - James; David Breckenridge - New Orleans; Rosalind Wyllie - Freshers; P.A. Tanton - Come Walk With Me On The Wild Side, Sweet Jesus; Steve Wheeler - The Good Provider.

Book of the Month - The Crack magazine, March 2006

Printed in the United Kingdom
by Lightning Source UK Ltd.
119763UK00001B/170